BEEZY MAGIC

stories by Megan McDonald
illustrated by Nancy Poydar

ORCHARD BOOKS   NEW YORK

Orchard Books, 95 Madison Avenue, New York, NY 10016

Manufactured in the United States of America
Printed by Barton Press, Inc. Bound by Horowitz/Rae
Book design by Mina Greenstein
The text of this book is set in 20 point Stempel Garamond.
The illustrations are gouache paintings reproduced in full color.
10 9 8 7 6 5 4 3 2 1

Library of Congress Cataloging-in-Publication Data
McDonald, Megan. Beezy magic / by Megan McDonald ;
illustrated by Nancy Poydar. p. cm.
Contents: Honeybee magic — Skinny-Minny Beanbag — Key lime pie.
Summary: Includes three episodes from the life of Beezy, who lives in
Florida with her best friend Merlin, Gran, and Funnybone.
ISBN 0-531-30064-1 (alk. paper). — ISBN 0-531-33064-8 (lib. bdg. : alk. paper)
[1. Best friends—Fiction.] I. Poydar, Nancy, ill. II. Title.
PZ7.M478419Bm 1998 [E]—dc21 97-24006

For Louise, Annie,
and Eliza

—M.M.

Contents

Honeybee Magic   7

Skinny-Minny Beanbag   19

Key Lime Pie   37

Honeybee Magic

"I hate my name," Beezy
told Merlin.
"Why do you hate your
name, Beezy?
Beezy is a good name."
"Not like Merlin," said Beezy.

"Merlin is a wizard.
Merlin means magic."
Merlin waved a stick in the
air like a magic wand.
"Tell me one good thing about
my name," said Beezy.

"One good thing about your
name is . . ."
Merlin scratched his head.
He scratched his ear.
"Well?"
"I'm thinking."
Merlin scratched his
mosquito bite.

"Beezy sounds like trees.

Beezy sounds like a bee.

Buzz. Buzz.

Beezy sounds like sneezy.

That is three good things."

"I'm going to change my name,"

said Beezy.

"Will I still be your best friend if you are not Beezy?"

"Yes, Merlin.

You will still be my best friend.

I will still be me.

I will still be Beezy.

But I will have a new name.

Like Rose. Or Wanda."

"But Rose is a flower," said Merlin.

"You are not a flower.

And Wanda is a dog I know.

A dog with fleas.

You are not a dog with fleas."

"Let's go tell Gran my new name is Rose."

Gran was painting the fence.

She asked, "What do you want
with a name like Rose
when you have your own
fine-sounding name?
Elizabeth. Elizabeth means
honeybee."

"Is that why you call me Beezy?"
"Remember the time
Merlin had a bee in his ear?"
asked Gran.
"And you put pepper up my
nose," said Merlin.

"I sneezed so hard,
I sneezed that bee right out of
my ear."

"You said just thinking about that
bee made you feel all 'beezy,' "
said Gran.
"We started calling you Beezy."
Beezy blinked.
She grinned at Merlin.
"I never knew my name means
honeybee."

Buzz, buzz, buzz.
Beezy buzzed in a circle
around Gran.
Buzz, buzz, buzz.

Beezy buzzed in a circle
around Merlin.
"Beezy has ants in her pants,"
said Merlin.

"Bees in her knees," Gran said.

"It's a dance," said Beezy.

Beezy spread her wings.

"Flight of the Honeybee."

Buzz, buzz, buzz.

"You will always be my honeybee," said Gran.

"You will always be my Beezy."

Skinny-Minny Beanbag

Sunday was bread day.

Beezy and Merlin helped Gran.

Beezy and Merlin got flour

on the floor.

On Funnybone.

In Beezy's hair.

Up Merlin's nose.

Even between their toes.

"Time for a story," said Gran.

Gran always told a story

while the bread rose.

They sat on the back steps.

Gran pulled a rabbit's foot
out of her pocket.

"This is a story about Rabbit
and how he fooled Panther.
One day, Rabbit found
Panther's teeth sitting on a log.

Rabbit stole the teeth.

He went to tell

Skinny-Minny Beanbag.

Skinny-Minny Beanbag

is an old rabbit.

She wears a bag around her neck.

It is not full of beans.

It is full of bones.

She lives down by the dark,

smelly swamp.

To get there you take the

Gumbo Limbo Trail

and cross the Kiss Me River.

To get there you have to
run some, swim some,

hide some, slip-slide some,
hop some, skip some, trip some,
and then some.

'Now Panther can't eat us,'
Rabbit said.

'You better watch out just the
same,' said Skinny-Minny
Beanbag.

Skinny-Minny Beanbag gave
Rabbit her lucky rabbit's foot.
'For good luck,' she said.
'Run all the way home.'
Rabbit ran.
Hip-hop, hip-hop, hip-hop, snap!
Rabbit's foot was in a trap.
'I got you, Rabbit,' said Panther.
'Now I'm going to eat you.'
'How will you eat me without
any teeth?'
'I'll gulp you down in one bite!'
'I won't taste good cold,'
said Rabbit.

'First you must build a fire.'

So Panther built a fire.

'Now you must do the
Stomp Dance.'

Panther stomped one foot,
then the other.

'Not like that,' said Rabbit.

'Show me how,' Panther said.

'I can't show you with my foot in this trap.'

'How do I know you'll put your foot back in the trap?'

'Fair is fair,' Rabbit said. 'I will put one foot back in the trap, or you can throw me into the Kiss Me River.'

'Fair is fair,' said Panther.

He snapped open the trap.

Rabbit did the Stomp Dance.

Hip-hop with one foot,

stomp-stomp-stomp with

the other.

Now Panther did the Stomp Dance.

'Put your foot back in that trap,'
Panther said.

'Keep dancing,' said Rabbit.

He took out the lucky rabbit's
foot and put it in the trap.

Rabbit said,

'Fair is fair.

I said I would put one foot in the trap, but I did not say which one.'
Panther stopped dancing.
'Fair is fair,' said Panther.
But he still picked Rabbit up by the ears and tossed him into the Kiss Me River.

Rabbit swam some, ran some, to
Skinny-Minny Beanbag's house.

'I lost your lucky rabbit's foot, but
I fooled Panther.'

He gave her Panther's teeth.
She put them in the bag
around her neck.
All but one.
'Keep one,' said Skinny-Minny
Beanbag. 'It will bring you good luck
on the way home.'

The end," Gran said.

"Time to go punch the bread."

"Did Rabbit make it home?"

asked Beezy.

"Yes," Gran said.

"Does your rabbit's foot

bring you good luck?"

Merlin asked.

"No," said Gran.

"But it brings me good stories."

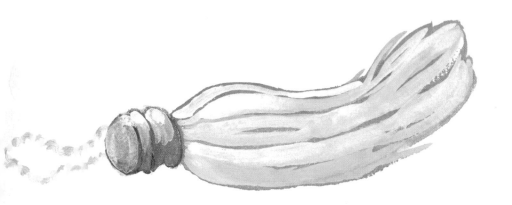

Key Lime Pie

"Eat your pancakes," Gran said.
"Today is a big day.
Today is your field trip
to the park."
"I get to ride the bus downtown
and have a cookout," said Beezy.

Funnybone licked Beezy's face.
"No, Funnybone," Beezy
told him.

"You are a D-O-G, dog.
Dogs cannot go on field trips."
Beezy put Funnybone on
his chain.
"Stay, Funnybone. Good dog."

Funnybone flopped
his tail.

Funnybone
drooped his ears.

"I will make it up to you.
I will go to the bake shop
and buy you a Key lime pie.
The thing you like best in all
the world."

Beezy and Merlin and Sarafina
rode the bus downtown.
Beezy forgot about Funnybone.

Funnybone tugged
at his chain.

Funnybone yanked his head
from side to side.
Funnybone broke
his collar!

Funnybone ran to the bus stop.

The bus was gone.

Funnybone ran to town.

He ran past the bank,
past the pet store,
past the bake shop.
Almost.

Funnybone saw something
in the window.
He wagged his tail.
It was not a ham bone.
It was not a dog bone.
It was a Key lime pie!
The thing he liked best
in all the world!
The door was open.
Funnybone knocked over
the NO PETS sign.
He knocked over a tray
of peanut butter cookies.

Funnybone jumped into
the bake shop window.

He licked up all the Key lime pie.

A lady with a mixing spoon
chased Funnybone around
the shop.
Funnybone ran.

The lady with the
spoon ran after him.

He ran and ran
all the way to the park.

"Funnybone!" said Beezy.
"How did you get here?"
Funnybone licked Beezy's face.
"He's green!" said Merlin.
"He's foaming at the mouth,"
Sarafina said.
"It's Key lime pie," said
the lady with the spoon.
"Bad dog!" said Beezy.

"I'm sorry," she told the lady.
"It's his favorite thing in all
the world."
"Key lime pie?" asked
Beezy's teacher.
"I'll have to buy one for my dog."
"Me too," said Ben's mother.
"Me too," Lucy's father said.

"This dog just sold three pies,"
said the lady with
the spoon.

"Good dog."
She patted Funnybone on the head.
Funnybone barked.
"Oh, Funnybone," said Beezy.
"You just had to have a field trip."

He ran after a butterfly.
He ate a hamburger
at the cookout
and rode the bus home
with Beezy.
"How was your field trip?"
Gran said.
"Ask Funnybone,"
said Beezy.